This book belongs to

_____

_____

_____

_____

Gleason, the Christmas Giraffe

by **Kay A. Eaton**

Illustrated by **Joshua Allen**

AuthorHouse™
1663 Liberty Drive, Suite 200
Bloomington, IN 47403
www.authorhouse.com
Phone: 1-800-839-8640

First published by AuthorHouse 5/7/2009

ISBN: 978-1-4389-3010-7 (sc)

Printed in the United States of America
Bloomington, Indiana

This book is printed on acid-free paper.

authorHOUSE®

Gleason was daydreaming again as he went on his daily hike to his favorite pond. Yesterday he imagined he was a monkey swinging from tree to tree and eating bananas, but today he was a pirate . . . *a very brave pirate.*

He covered one eye with his hoof, pretending he had a patch, and with the other hoof he picked up a stick and began swinging it around like a sword.

"Take that! And that! And that!" he yelled as he stabbed at and destroyed his imaginary enemy.

With his head held high, he strutted proudly. Once again he was the hero . . . *a strong and handsome hero.*

As he skipped along, he was unaware of the real adventure that was about to take place.

Arriving at the small lake, he stretched his legs far apart, lowered his long neck, and began to drink the refreshing water.

Suddenly Gleason heard a strange noise. Was his imagination playing tricks on him? It sounded like someone sawing logs.

Slowly he raised his head and peeked through his long eyelashes.

SNORE! SNORE!

There it was again!

He turned his head toward the noise.

What is this? Gleason thought to himself as he tiptoed toward the strange sight.

Earlier that day, Santa and his reindeer had decided to stop for a nap in Africa. The reindeer enjoyed a snack of tender green grass, drank from the pond, and soon joined Santa in slumber.

Sleeping soundly, all the reindeer were unaware of the approaching young giraffe.

What is this? Who are they? Why are they here? And what's that strange noise? Gleason thought to himself.

He stepped gently around the reindeer and approached the object under the tree. It was a man all dressed in red, and he was sound asleep.

SNORE! SNORE!

3

Gleason covered his ears and ran as fast as he could to get away. He stumbled, trying to avoid stepping on the reindeer, and fell against the sleigh. His heart was pounding rapidly and his eyes were as wide as could be, but the man in the red clothes continued to sleep. As he regained his balance, his heart slowly returned to its normal beat.

That's when he saw it! A gigantic bag! The biggest bag he had ever seen was in the back of the sleigh! What could be in such a huge bag?

Gleason's curiosity took over. Ignoring the warning he heard in his head, he stretched his l-o-n-g neck as far as it would go and peeked into the bag.

TOYS! Gleason thought to himself. *Lots and lots of toys!*

He couldn't believe his eyes! He just had to see every one of them! Dare he get into the sleigh?

Gleason looked at that snoring man again. The reindeer were also sound asleep.

Just a quick look, he thought, *and I'll leave before anyone wakes up.*

Silently, Gleason slid into the sleigh. Why, this bag was big enough for him to climb in — so he did!

The toys were beyond anything young Gleason had ever dreamed. He was so delighted with his newfound treasure that he forgot all about the man in the red suit and the snoozing reindeer.

He didn't know how much time had passed, but suddenly he was aware of a great deal of commotion. Someone was shouting!

Waking up, Santa realized that they had stayed too long and it would be nearly impossible to get all the toys delivered in time for Christmas!

"Wake up! We're going to be late," he yelled.

The reindeer jumped into place just as Santa cracked the whip.

Instantly they were in the air and on their way to deliver toys.

Gleason was hardly breathing! What was happening? Where were they going?

After some time he heard Santa breathe a deep sigh. Smiling, he said, "Good job. We did it! Let's head for home."

Home? thought Gleason. *Good. As soon as this sleigh lands I'll be out of here so fast they'll never know I was here!*

Thinking he was home, he was surprised to find he was getting cold . . . *very cold!* He had never been this cold before. Where was he? Slowly, he realized that they must be far away from his home.

"There's our Star. Follow it home," he heard Santa say.

If Gleason had been brave enough to peek out of the bag, he would have seen a dark sky full of stars. But there was one Star that was bigger and brighter than all the others.

The elves greeted Santa as the sleigh landed safely.

Winking at the reindeer, Santa said, "That was a close one, but we delivered all the toys on time and still enjoyed a good nap in Africa."

He turned to the waiting elves. They had finished their live Nativity and were still dressed in their costumes.

"Thanks for our Star. We could never get home without it," Santa said. "Take it down from the crane and put the sleigh in the shed. We'll save clean-up for tomorrow."

Gleason was scared and cold . . . *very cold!* Tears came to his eyes. How was he going to get home? He didn't even know where he was! He shivered and pulled the now empty bag closer to him hoping to get warm.

It was the longest night of his short life.

When morning came, Gleason decided to check out his surroundings and make a plan for getting home.

The sleigh shed was quiet.

Gleason pulled the toy bag closer to him. Just as he was about to step out of the sleigh, the doors flew open.

A wide-eyed giraffe and a wide-eyed elf stared at each other. They both screamed! Gleason bumped his head on the ceiling and dropped to the floor, pulling the bag over himself in an attempt to hide from the elf who was dashing out the door.

"SANTA!" yelled Conrad.

Gleason began to tremble when he heard Santa enter the shed.

Santa looked at the shaking bag. "Come on out. Don't be afraid."

He looked at the huge animal in amazement. "Well, Mr. Giraffe, who are you, and how did you come to be in my sleigh shed?"

"M-m-my name is G-Gl-Gleason." He wasn't sure if he was stammering because he was scared or because he was cold . . . *very cold.*

"I - I climbed into your toy bag while you were sleeping. I didn't mean to cause trouble. I just wanted to see the toys, and then, well, next thing I knew, well . . . well, here I am. I don't know where I am or how to get home."

Santa thought for a moment. "Well, to answer your first question, you're at the North Pole, and to answer your next question . . ." Santa began pacing back and forth.

"Getting you home is a real challenge. My reindeer only fly at Christmastime, and . . . and . . . Christmas is over."

Gleason's big eyes got bigger! "You mean, you mean I can't go home?"

"Well, yes, but . . . but not till next year," Santa said softly.

"NEXT YEAR!" Gleason couldn't believe his big ears! "Can't I just walk back home? I have long legs and run really fast."

"No, Gleason. It's impossible. But, we'll take good care of you, and next Christmas will be here before you know it," assured Santa. "However, I think the first thing we must do is get you some warm clothes."

Santa spoke to the elf hiding behind him. "Conrad, go find your twin sister, Connie, and see what you can find to fit Gleason. Look how cold he is . . . *very cold.*"

Conquering his fear of the big giraffe, Conrad motioned for Gleason to follow him.

Still wrapped in the toy bag, Gleason lowered his long neck through the door and followed Conrad into the snow.

SNOW! Gleason had never seen snow before! Brrrrr! It was cold . . . *very cold!*

Conrad laughed as Gleason stumbled and fell face-first in the snow.

When Gleason raised his head, all he could see was the pile of snow on the end of his nose. He shook his head, and the white flakes landed on Conrad! Now they were both laughing. The other elves came out to see what was happening.

In between laughs, Conrad introduced Gleason to the group of onlookers.

"Wow! A giraffe! A real live giraffe!" cried the elves, jumping up and down.

"As you can see," said Conrad, "Gleason is cold . . . *very cold* . . . and he needs warm clothes."

Immediately the elves scampered off to see what they could find.

The twin elves escorted Gleason into the Toy Shop and sat him by the fireplace. His shivering soon stopped.

"Where are we?" he asked.

"This is the Toy Shop where we make all the toys for Christmas," answered Connie.

"But the shelves are empty," replied Gleason.

"Before next Christmas," Connie said, "the shelves will be loaded with new toys."

"You mean like the toys I saw in the bag? I love toys! Will you show me how to make them?" Gleason asked.

"We are all expert toy-makers," Conrad said proudly, "but I'm sure there's a job for you."

Just then the elves returned bringing their own clothes for Gleason. There were shoes, boots, socks, pants, shirts, sweaters, gloves, scarves, and even earmuffs.

As they looked down at the pile of clothes at Gleason's feet, they realized that these clothes would never fit a giraffe! He was so big! And they were so small!

"If we can make toys, we can make clothes," Connie said. "Get the patterns for the doll clothes, and we'll just make them bigger . . . *a lot bigger!*"

The elves measured Gleason from head to hoof, and soon everyone was busy cutting, sewing, and knitting. Before long, Gleason was showing off his new winter clothes. The pants were too short, and the sleeves were too long, but the boots were a perfect fit.

A big cheer went up when Gleason put on the earmuffs, and they proudly escorted him outside to introduce him to the reindeer.

When Gleason and the elves weren't busy making toys, they were having great adventures playing in the snow. The elves taught Gleason the fine art of having snowball fights and how to build snow forts. But their favorite game was sliding down his long neck and landing in snowdrifts!

Over time Gleason became an excellent ice skater, but he was happiest in the Toy Shop. Everyone had their assigned task. It was Gleason's job to put the toys on the shelves. He took great pride in carefully placing each toy in its proper place.

The days and weeks went by quickly. Shortly before Christmas, Conrad and Connie asked Gleason to help get things ready for the Nativity.

"What's a Nativity?" Gleason asked.

"Every year while Santa is delivering toys, we set up the stable and dress like shepherds, wise men, angels, Mary, and Joseph, just like in the Christmas story," explained Conrad. "One of the elves operates the crane that holds our Star over the stable."

He continued, "While Connie reads the Christmas story, we act it out. When we finish, we leave our Star in place and Santa uses it to find his way home."

"Will you tell me the Christmas story?" asked Gleason.

15

"Christmas is when we celebrate God sending his Son to earth. He came as a baby to Mary and Joseph, and his name was Jesus. When he was born, angels made the announcement to shepherds who were taking care of sheep. The angels told them to go to Bethlehem where they would find the baby. The sky filled up with more angels than you could count. When the shepherds found the baby Jesus, they worshiped him."

Gleason pointed to the Star propped up in the corner. "What about that Star?"

"A special Star led wise men to Bethlehem. When they found Jesus, they gave him gifts. That's why we give gifts today. We can't give them directly to Jesus, so we give them to each other."

Gleason was getting more excited with every passing day. It was almost time for Christmas, and soon he would be going home.

Finally it was Christmas Eve!

Surrounded by all the elves dressed in their Nativity costumes, Gleason began to say his good-byes. Conrad and Connie tried to be cheerful, but tears spilled down their faces. Gleason scooped them up in his long legs and hugged them as best he could.

"We'll always be friends," he whispered to them.

Santa was already in the sleigh when one of the elves came running up to them.

"Santa! Santa! The crane is broken!"

Everyone gasped! Broken! How would they get their Star up? How would Santa get back home?

"What are we going to do? How are we going to get our Star high enough without the crane?" the elf cried.

Everyone was silent.

Gleason had already climbed into the sleigh and was eager to get started when he realized they were all looking at him.

"Wh - What?"

They were looking at his l-o-n-g . . . *very long* . . . neck.

"Why are you looking at me? I - I'm going h - home," stammered Gleason.

"But, but Gleason," Conrad said slowly, "Santa depends on our Star."

Gleason knew he was the only one who could help, but his heart was set on going home. He had been gone a whole year and if he stayed it would be another year before he could leave. If he left now, Santa wouldn't be able to find the North Pole and that would mean there may never be another Christmas . . . but, if he stayed . . . Gleason couldn't bear to finish his thought.

They were counting on him. He needed to stay. With sad eyes he slowly stepped out of the sleigh and headed for the shed to get the Star.

"Thank you, Gleason," Santa whispered. "Somehow we will make it up to you."

Gleason looked back over his shoulder and watched as the sleigh lifted in the air. He blinked back the tears.

Quietly the elves took their places in the manger scene as Gleason lifted up the Star. Connie began to read the Christmas story. "There were shepherds in a nearby field . . ."

When the story ended, the elves gathered silently around Gleason and waited quietly. They didn't want to leave their friend alone.

After a long time Conrad shouted, "There's Santa! He's back!"

Gleason tried to smile as the elves cheered, but he was sad . . . *very sad.*

As he lay down that night, he dreamed of home. Home . . . where it was warm!

While Gleason slept, the elves began to pray. "Dear God, Gleason made a sacrifice tonight so that Santa could find his way home. Please help him."

In his dream Gleason could smell the grass . . . *the elves continued to pray. . .* the sun was warm on his back . . . *the elves were still praying . . .* he felt as if he were floating.

While Gleason was dreaming, unseen by anyone, angels gently cradled him in their wings. Without making a sound they moved across the heavens and tenderly placed him in the fresh green grass by the pond near his home.

His dream was so real! He thought he heard his name being called.

"Gleason! Gleason!"

It sounded like his family! He squeezed his eyes shut as hard as he could! It was such a wonderful dream he didn't want to wake up!

"Gleason! Gleason!"

His eyes flew open! Was it true?

"Am I . . . am I really home? How did I get here?" he asked.

The angels smiled.

And Gleason was warm . . . *very warm.*

CPSIA information can be obtained
at www.ICGtesting.com
Printed in the USA
LVRC020452281018
594835LV00001B/7